WORLD OF ERIC CARLE
An imprint of Penguin Random House LLC, New York

First published in the United States of America by World of Eric Carle,
an imprint of Penguin Random House LLC, New York, 2023

Words by Gabriella DeGennaro

To find out more about Eric Carle and his books, please visit eric-carle.com.
To learn about The Eric Carle Museum of Picture Book Art, please visit carlemuseum.org.

Visit us online at penguinrandomhouse.com.

Library of Congress Cataloging-in-Publication Data is available.

Manufactured in China

ISBN 9780593523155

10 9 8 7 6 5 4 3 2 HH

I ♥ GRANDMA

with The Very Hungry Caterpillar

world of
ERIC
CARLE™

Grandma...

I look up to you.

You're kind,

patient,

and so very
strong.

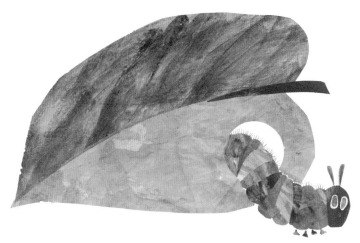

Even when . . .

we're **apart,**

and I'm feeling
blue,

you remind me to look on the **bright** side.

When we're

together...

we make the

perfect **pair.**

That's **why...**

I  GRAN

YOU

OMA